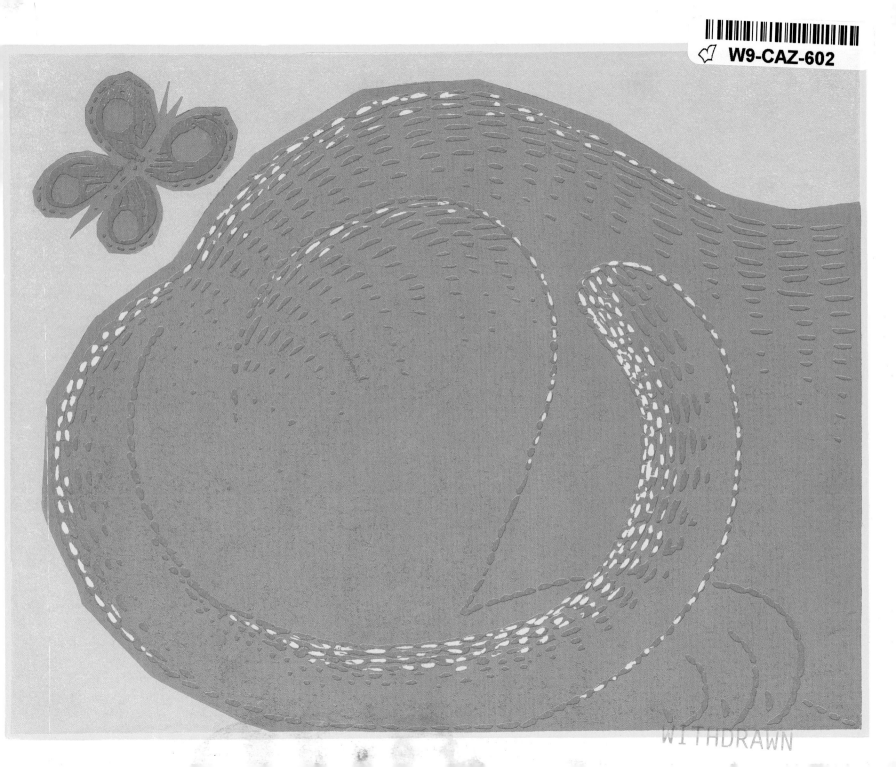

My Beastie Book of

HarperCollinsPublishers

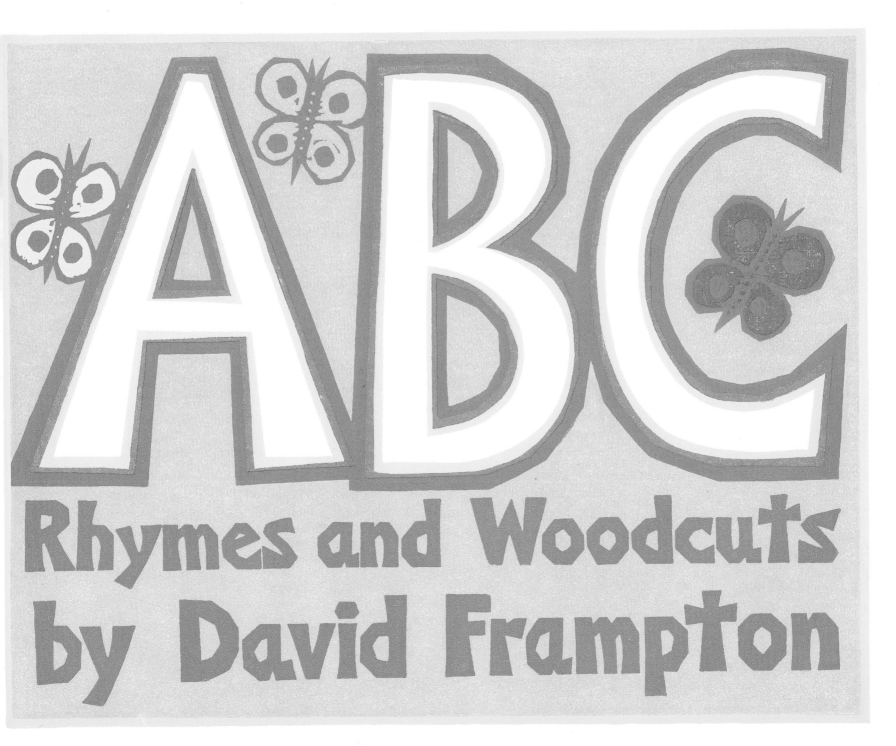

ABC

Rhymes and Woodcuts
by David Frampton

A is for alligator. Her teeth are quite awesome. Yours will be too, if you just brush and floss 'em.

B is for butterflies
up in the sky,
like silky bow ties
all fluttering by.

D is for dinosaur, not found at the zoo or anywhere else....boo hoo!

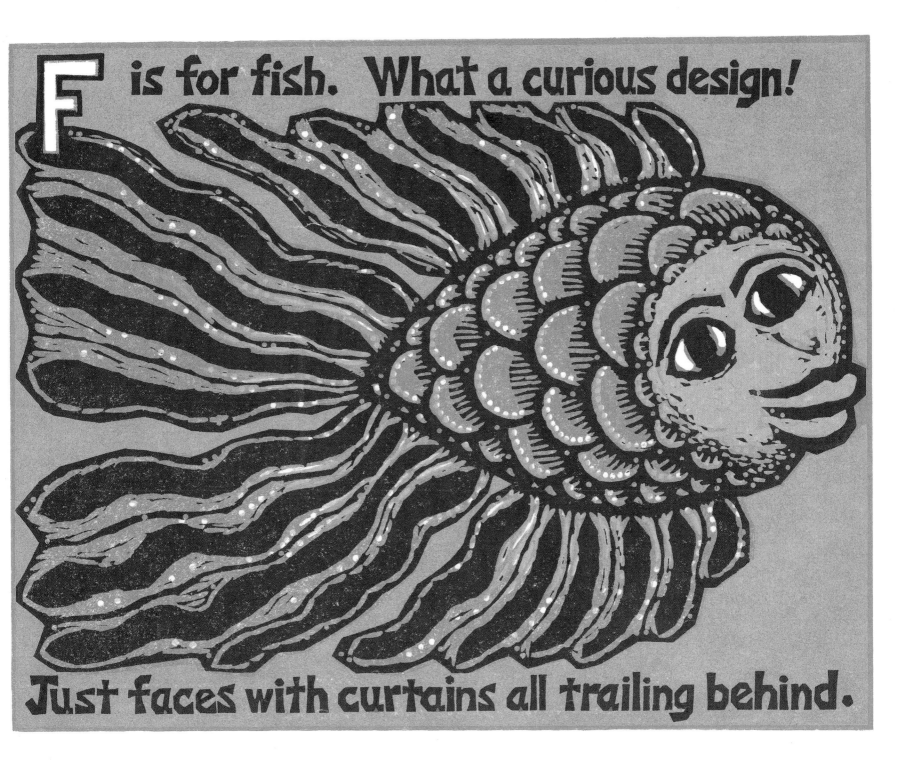

G is for grasshopper,
up down and up,
over your sandwich
into your cup.

H is for hippo with mouth open wide. You could easily fit a tricycle inside. But then, it might be too yucky to ride.

I is for iguana.

I have one named Donna.
You can have one too,
unless you don't wanna.

V is for vulture. They dine on decay.
A truly disgusting and smelly buffet.
But better than broccoli any old day!

Z is for zebra with stripes which of course is a very good way to tell them from horses.

For my children, Sarah and David, who have given me so much help on this book

My Beastie Book of ABC
Copyright © 2002 by David Frampton
Printed in the U.S.A. All rights reserved.
www.harperchildrens.com

Library of Congress Cataloging-in-Publication Data
Frampton, David.
  My beastie book of ABC : rhymes and woodcuts / by David Frampton.
      p.   cm.
  Summary: Illustrations and brief rhymes present an alphabet of
animals from alligator and hippo to parrot and zebra.
  ISBN 0-06-028824-8 (lib. bdg.) — ISBN 0-06-028823-X
  1. Animals—Juvenile poetry. 2. Children's poetry, American. 3. Alphabet
rhymes. [1. Animals—Poetry. 2. American poetry. 3. Alphabet.] I. Title.
PS3606.R36 M9 2002   2001039220
811'.54—dc21   CIP
                                                          AC

1 2 3 4 5 6 7 8 9 10
❖
First Edition